The
Little Red Buckets

The
Little Red Buckets

Lynda M. Nelson

A Perigee Book

A Perigee Book
Published by The Berkley Publishing Group
A member of Penguin Putnam Inc.
200 Madison Avenue
New York, NY 10016

Copyright © 1995 by Lynda M. Nelson
Book design by Jill Dinneen
Interior illustrations on pages 97, 98, 105, 106, 115, and 116 by V. Gail
Pierson; all other illustrations by Patrick Caldwell

Galleon Publications edition published 1995
First Perigee edition: November 1997

Published simultaneously in Canada.

The Putnam Berkley World Wide Web site address is
http://www.berkley.com

Library of Congress Cataloging-in-Publication Data
Nelson, Lynda.
    The little red buckets/Lynda M. Nelson.—1st Perigee ed.
        p.   cm.
    "A Perigee book."
    Summary: Grandmother tells the story of carrying buckets of food as a
child to an elderly neighbor, who rewards her with the gift of a crystal figure
with a guardian angel attached.
    ISBN 0-399-52357-X
    [1. Sharing—Fiction.   2. Pails—Fiction.   3. Angels—Fiction.
4. Grandmothers—Fiction].   Title.
PZ7.N4346Li   1997
[Fic]—dc21   97-6696
                                                                      CIP
                                                                       AC

Printed in the United States of America

10   9   8   7   6   5   4   3   2   1

To Mark
for always believing

For my very own angels,
Chantal, Amber, and Kelly

The
Little Red Buckets

Grandma Jenny

Punch! Rolllll! Slap! Slap! Rolllll! Flour rose above the sturdy white-painted wooden table in little puffy clouds. Grandmother was making homemade bread. Sarah watched as the weathered hands, looking years younger with their powdering of white flour, expertly flipped, worked, and rolled the soft dough. Then they deftly molded it into three loaves and plopped them into the old and dented bread pans.

"Grandma Jenny," questioned the little girl, "how did you learn to make homemade bread so well?" Sarah's dainty hands, gooey and sticky from her own

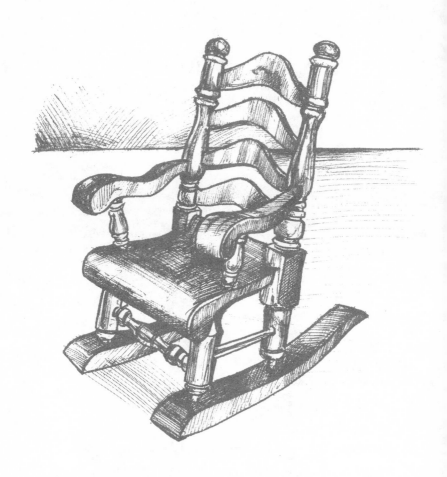

bread-making, carefully rolled her bit of dough into a small loaf and placed it gently in a miniature bread pan. However, when she tried to let go of the dough, it stuck stubbornly to her little fingers. Sarah furiously wiggled and flicked her fingers until the little ball of bread dough finally dropped—half in and half out of the pan. Grandma watched sympathetically, her lips moving. Whenever she concentrated, one side of Grandma's mouth worked back and forth into a pucker, as if a thread inside was being pulled and released, her eyes squinting brightly behind silver spectacles.

"Mamma makes bread sometimes, but hers isn't nearly as good as yours," Sarah earnestly continued her conversation. The wild uncontrollable temper usually associated with red-headed children was totally absent in Sarah. Though her hair was the shade of rich, red auburn, and her creamy white nose and cheeks were liberally sprinkled with delicate freckles, her blue eyes more often sparkled with laughter and kindness than anger.

The plump little lady laughed at her granddaughter and Sarah looked up and smiled. Sarah loved Grandma's laugh. It was a high falsetto, like a rich soprano. When Grandma laughed, Sarah couldn't resist laughing too because Grandma's more-than-ample tummy jiggled delightfully, and Sarah found that amusing.

"Cover your hands with flour, Sarah, my angel, and the dough won't stick to them quite so much." Grandma Jenny watched Sarah work and her own skilled hands were still for a moment. "Well, sweetie, your mama didn't get as much practice as I did at making bread. When I was ten, my mother—your great-grandmother Perry—put me to making bread. We had to make six loaves every two days to feed our family, occasional visitors, and some for the sick folk."

Sarah glanced up as Grandma's impish green eyes behind the round, wire-rimmed glasses stared out the window above the cast iron sink, its chipped enamel well scrubbed. Down the hill from that side of the cabin, Sarah knew, was Grandma's raspberry patch, hidden amongst the wild forest, but surrounded with a quaint, picturesque pole fence. A faraway look came over Grandma's face, a look Sarah had seen there many times before.

"Hmm, so many loaves of bread—I don't even think about it anymore. Making bread is just part of my life." Sarah could tell her grandmother was off thinking in the past again so she concentrated on her stubborn, sticky little loaf of bread dough and patiently waited to see what would come from this nostalgic, mental journey.

Grandma raised her finely arched eyebrows and tilted her head a bit to one side, with her arms crossed beneath her ample bosom. Black-peppered silver curls lay neatly against her head, held tightly in place by a finely woven black hair net. Grandma Jenny lifted one hand and tapped a floured finger against her soft, wrinkled cheek. "I was born in 1908, so that means I've been making bread for the better part of sixty-seven years now."

The slim, silver wedding band on Grandma's left hand flashed in the bright sunshine as she turned back to the table, reached out and gently patted the white loaves. "My goodness, but that's a long time."

Grandma Jenny gazed out through the small picture window at the front of the cabin. Tall evergreen trees rose majestically above leafless bushes and mingled their rich color with the bare, black and white stands of quaking aspens on the opposite hillside rising from her narrow valley. Grandpa Jack was high up inside that mountain, still stubbornly blasting and chiseling coal from the dark recesses of their mine.

"Look, Grandma, my loaf is all ready to cook." Sarah proudly held up her little bread pan for Grandma's inspection, gently calling her attention back to the present. The top of the little loaf had ripples and dents, and one end was taller and broader than the other.

A mischievous smile lit up Grandma Jenny's face and her eyes twinkled with suppressed laughter. "That loaf is simply loaded with personality and by far the best loaf ever made by an eight-year-old girl. Wait till you're fourteen, you'll be making them with your eyes shut. By the time I was fourteen years old, I could make bread while dreaming of the handsome prince who'd ride up on a white horse and carry me away to his castle someday."

Two dimples peeped out in Sarah's cheeks as she giggled at the thought of Grandma and a handsome prince on a white horse. "Grandma? Did the prince really come and carry you away?"

"He sure did, Sarah honey, only the horse was black, and the prince was named Jack. When he rode up, I curtsied just like a princess." With one hand lightly holding out the skirt of her flowered kitchen dress, Grandma Jenny performed a graceful curtsey.

"Then we danced." Straightening back up, she grasped Sarah by her little hand and twirled her around and around. When she stopped, Sarah was just a bit dizzy and quickly stepped sideways to keep from falling over. It was easy to laugh at Grandma's house.

"But that's not the story I'm going to tell you today, my darling little angel." Grandma Jenny left Sarah to catch her balance while she lifted the bread pans, one by one, onto the warming shelf above the old black, coal-burning stove and draped a clean white towel over the top of the three large pans and the one small pan.

"C'mere, Sarah, darlin', let's clean our hands off, then I'll tell you a story about when I was just your age." Grandma Jenny wiped the flour from her hands. Then she untied and removed her white, full length apron, and hung it on a peg beside the sink. Sarah took a bit longer to rub the remnants of sticky dough from her small fingers. When she finally turned from the sink, holding up her clean hands for inspection, Grandma had already pulled her old rocking chair into the center of the small kitchen and sat down. Her gaily flowered dress, nylons rolled down to her ankles, and sturdy black support shoes made Grandma eminently loveable and touchable.

"I'm sure glad Mother let me stay with you this weekend, Grandma." Sarah climbed carefully onto her grandmother's lap because, after all, she was almost nine years old and she was a big girl now. A tiny, unformed thought of gratitude flitted through Sarah's mind, unbidden, that the rocking chair was sturdy enough to support them both.

Originally fashioned from white oak, years of polish and frequent use had left the smooth old chair burnished a rich golden hue. It was Grandma's most elegant piece of furniture. Grandpa Jack had carved and fashioned it for Jenny as a wedding present and its timeless beauty lent an air of elegance to the room filled with antiques that were still in daily use. When Grandma sat down, the chair creaked and groaned, as though to welcome the familiar form to its loving embrace. The November sunshine beaming through the window emphasized the lighter parts of the wood in the chair arms while casting the rocker feet into deep mahogany shadows.

Heat radiated from the ornate coal stove, giving the old mining cabin nestled deep in Huntington Canyon a homey warmth. Three hand-made rag rugs added their bright colors to the flowered green linoleum covering the floor. Though old and cracked, the linoleum was clean and polished, adding a rich sense of days long past, eloquently recording a long life filled with work and love, sadness and joy.

The other furniture consisted of an old naugahyde couch where Sarah slept when she stayed at Grandma's cabin, four unmatched table chairs, and two white china hutches built into the walls at either side of the front window. Through the glass doors stood an array of china and different colored glass dishware. In the cupboard to the left of the window was a partial set of deep green, cut-glass bowls, plates and cups. The one on the right revealed shiny peach-colored glass plates, platters, bowls and cups. Clear, cut-crystal sugar, cream and candy bowls sparkled delightfully, spraying prisms of colored light across the white ceiling and flower-papered walls. Investigating Grandma Jenny's dishes provided a mysterious adventure for her little grand-daughter. Sarah lived in a modern house in a large city and visiting Grandma was like stepping back in time a full century.

Grandma Jenny always had the best stories to tell of when she was small. Life for a little girl was different back then and Sarah could listen for hours to stories of those long ago days. With a sigh of deep contentment, Sarah snuggled close to her Grandmother's portly form and laid her head lovingly on the sweetly scented shoulder. Grandma always wore a perfume called Lavender, and breathing deeply, Sarah closed her bright blue eyes contentedly and reveled in the familiar aromas. Burning coal, fresh bread, and lavender—those were smells that meant Grandma Jenny, and Grandma Jenny meant love.

The Little Red Buckets

 Two doughy-soft arms wrapped Sarah in a loving embrace and the chair began to rock slowly back and forth. The soft creaking was echoed by crackling and popping coming from the fire in the stove.

"Do you see those four little red tin buckets sitting up on the shelf way up above my old stove?" Grandma asked.

Sarah raised her head a bit and looked carefully at the contents of the shelf high up near the ceiling. "The ones that say 'Pure Lard' on the side?" read Sarah.

"Mm hmm. They've got pinyon nuts in them right

now, but when I was little we used those little red buckets for all sorts of things. Tin buckets were a hard item to come by back then. So my father, George Perry, handmade most of our buckets from wooden slats. But those red lard buckets came straight from the store. Once the lard was used up out of 'em, we washed and saved them and used 'em to carry seeds at planting time, chicken feed in the morning and evening, peas and beans when the garden was ready—we used them any old which way 'til they were plumb tuckered out.

"When Mother and Zella and I had dinged and beaten and bent up them little buckets, my father and brother Ralph would take 'em to use around the farm. Rings of red tin hammered to the trunks kept the squirrels and mice from climbing up our fruit trees and eating the apples and cherries and peaches. The scarecrows in our fields and garden had wind chimes made from that red tin to help keep hungry birds out of our crops. My father even nailed a piece of that red tin to a horse's hoof once where it had split out. He said the tin acted like a bandage for the hoof, holding the edges together 'til the split could grow out and be clipped off."

Sarah gazed with renewed interest at the old red buckets. She had often seen them before, enjoying their bright color amongst all the other interesting objects in Grandma's kitchen. Sarah's attention wandered a moment, while her eyes meandered over the other items on the carved wooden shelf.

There was Grandpa Jack's mysterious sea-green-colored glass gallon jug. Inside it were different colored rocks covering the bottom and it was filled to the top with water. Grandpa drank some of that water every day before walking up to the coal mine. Sarah had watched him many times and it gave her the shivers to see him do it. Grandpa called it mineral water and often spoke of its medicinal qualities. He always offered Sarah a glass, but she never dared to even take a sip. She was secretly waiting for the day that some slithery sea creature would stare out at her from the rocks; but none ever did. Sarah was almost disappointed.

Hanging from a nail on the shelf was the battered white colander Grandma used to strain her homemade noodles. It was old as well, but there was just a hint of the strawberry pattern on white enamel which had decorated the colander when it was new. Also on the shelf were big colored bottles of rose, blue, lavender, and green—some round, some curved, some square. Most held things like dried beans and peas, rose hips, currants, raisins, and nuts. Two oil lanterns with tall glass chimneys sat gracefully on the far end of the shelf next to a mason jar full of crystal rock candies. Sarah's roving eyes took in the flowered metal box hanging on the wall by the stove which held a new box of matches and a small cup to hold the burnt ones.

Four large geraniums, growing in glorious abandon, bloomed proudly and brightly in the southern window. The low November sun and the warmth of Grandma's house produced beautiful red, pink, and magenta blossoms. Grandma dearly loved flowers, their fragrance, their color, their life.

These familiar sights and smells added to Sarah's feeling of deep contentment. She reached a small arm up to wrap around her grandmother's neck, then planted an affectionate kiss on her Grandmother's soft, powdery cheek. In a world distracted by its appetite for newer and better things, Grandma's home provided a safe haven. To Sarah, Grandma's house never seemed to change and she loved it for the comfort of stable security.

"We only went to the store once a month, less in the wintertime." Grandma gently placed a rosy lipstick kiss on Sarah's smooth little forehead. Then she proceeded with her story, holding her precious grandchild and rocking contentedly.

"It was pretty much a full day affair to go to the store when I was little. Oh, my goodness, how we did look forward to those trips. There was no television or radio in those days. Any news we received about the big, wide world outside our valley came from a few visitors from time t' time, an occasional newspaper which was usually weeks old when we finally got it, and our trips to the country store.

"We girls always dressed up a bit, tied ribbons in our hair and wore our second-best dresses. Zella and I were the same height, even though she was older. I was stocky and she was thin as a rail fence, but we could still share dresses. My face was round and hers was long and narrow. Our hair was the same color, but my eyes were green and hers were hazel. Zella was a spitfire with a quick temper and a sharp tongue. We were different in so many ways and we argued constantly. But through it all we were sisters, and we loved each other.

Zella was . . . oh, oops. I got sidetracked again, didn't I, Sarah?"

"Yes, Grandma, but you're forgiven. You were talking about going to the country store and getting all dressed up." Sarah stifled a mischievous giggle.

"Thank you, Sarah, what would I do without you to keep my memory straight. Well, let's see. Ralph, our brother, would shine his boots and wear his best black hat and turquoise neckerchief. During the wagon ride to town Zella and I would tussle around in the back of the wagon, laughing and arguing, too excited to sit quiet. Ralph always rode his horse to town, sometimes riding beside the wagon, sometimes way up ahead. He often performed tricks on his horse to entertain us during those long, bumpy, dusty rides.

"Bo, his horse, was a patient old soul. He just trotted or galloped along in a straight line while Ralph jumped up and down, stood in the saddle, rode backwards, sideways, and upside down. The few times that Ralph missed his hold and fell, Zella and I laughed 'til our sides split, for old Bo would stop and turn his head around to look back at Ralph sprawled in the dirt. Then he would raise his upper lip and wiggle it at

Ralph. That was Bo's way of laughing at Ralph for falling off.

"When we finally rumbled and rattled to the out-skirts of town, Zella and I would tumble out of the wagon and race around the few buildings to see if any of our friends were in town too. There would usually be at least one or two and the bunch of us spent several hours laughing and talking, and playing games. Ralph often found several of his friends in town as well. Some of the younger boys occasionally got into arguments and once in awhile there'd be a fist fight. Ralph and his friends gave a few boxing lessons and cheered the young fellows on, but they were usually the ones who broke up the fights before the parents got wind of 'em. Those days were pretty exciting.

"We knew that when we got hungry, we'd find Father standing around the feed store or the livery sta-ble, talking to any of the other menfolk who happened to be in town. Mother would spend her day chatting with the storekeeper's wife. They were very good friends. They also traded stories with any other women who came in and out of the store and of course chased all of the children away from the candy bottles.

"I still remember walking around Mr. Maeser's store, listening to the ladies talking, sniffing at the rich aromas of coffee, onions, leather, grease, and bolts of fabric. In one corner was a cupboard full of spice bottles. It was a magical corner, for those bottles gave off the most mysterious aroma of cinnamon, nutmeg, cloves, and sharp curry. Most intriguing, however, was the candy counter with its bright colors and tantalizing flavors. Tall glass bottles stood on the countertop, filled with sweet treasures—lemon drops, licorice, hard tack, peppermints, suckers, and chocolates." Grandma's hands painted a picture in the air as she spoke of the candy counter.

"My father would trade wheat for ground flour at the mill and once a year he'd trade a plump pig and a couple of fattened steers to Mr. Maeser on account. That way we had credit throughout the year which we used to buy things we couldn't make for ourselves on the farm. Zella and I got to divide up the eggs I collected for the two days before our trips to town and we would trade the eggs for things that we wanted to purchase at the store. We usually used all our credit to purchase a small brown bag full of candy for just ourselves.

And along with all the other supplies Mother brought home each month were a few of those shiny red buckets full of lard."

"What's lard, Grandma?" asked Sarah.

Grandma stopped rocking for just a moment and shifted her position in the rocking chair. Once comfortable, she started rocking again as she answered Sarah's question.

"Folks don't use lard much anymore. Too much fat. That lard was what we used for short'nin' back in those days for making bread and cookies, and for cookin' fried taters and such. It was pure white and looked like snow when we opened those little red buckets."

"Then, when the buckets were empty, we used most of 'em around the farm for the chores I told you about. But my mother always saved a few of those little red buckets for special occasions, like Christmas."

Grandma Jenny stopped rocking again, lifted Sarah gently off her lap and stood up.

"Is that the end of the story, Grandma?" There was great disappointment in Sarah's tiny voice.

"Oh, no, that's just the very beginning," laughed

Grandma. "But I figured you would need a cookie or two to munch on while I tell it."

Grandma ambled over to the cupboard beside the sink, stretching out a kink in her back on the way. She opened a white cupboard door, reached inside and pulled out a red bucket. When she had pried the lid off, Sarah saw that it was full of chocolate chip cookies. Grandma set the open bucket on the table near their chair, then sat back down. Sarah climbed back into her lap and snuggled close, but not before she picked up a handful of chocolate chip cookies. Nestled contentedly against Grandma's shoulder, munching hungrily, Sarah kept her bright blue eyes focused on the red buckets up on the shelf.

The aroma of rising bread and warm pinyon nuts permeated the cozy kitchen and wrapped Sarah in a wonderful, peaceful feeling as she listened to her Grandmother Jenny start her story.

The Hill

 "A very poor couple moved into a small tarpaper shack up the hill from our farm when I was just eight years old. They were nice old people, Mr. and Mrs. Nie, and they'd seen a lot of hard times. Mr. Nie was a very hard worker, but his luck just seemed to run to the bad side. Well, my father and mother, being true Christians, took it upon themselves to help the Nies.

"Though Mr. Nie was too old to do heavy work anymore, it didn't take Father long to discover that he was still a skilled leather craftsman and wood carver. Now, Father wanted to help these people, and he didn't

want to offend their sense of pride by just giving them food and supplies. But he couldn't stand by and watch them starve, either. So Father hired Mr. Nie to carve a big sign to hang over the entrance to our farmyard, and when he had finished that, Father found other odd jobs he could hire Mr. Nie to do.

"Before you knew it, we had carved wooden signs over the chicken coop and the milking barn, the tack shed and even over all the horse stalls. In time, we had new harnesses to replace the worn out pieces for the plowing and pulling teams, and Mother's old wooden trunk received new leather straps. There even came to be a sign bearing our family name standing out at the main road, some two miles away with an arrow pointing up our road toward the house. All these things my father hired Mr. Nie to make for us. I think the signs were things my father always wanted to have, but didn't have the time to make, what with all the farm work he and my brother, Ralph, had to do.

"We lived in a little valley in the hills, deep in the vast expanse of the Uintah mountain range. Our farm lay on the east side of the valley and was set right up at the base of the foothills. A colorful patchwork of farm fields and green animal pastures spread out in front of the house while wooded hills rose behind it. A sparkling stream, slowed by an occasional beaver pond, gurgled over stones and around boulders, coming out of the high mountains to the north of our house, and flowed happily past our barn and corral. From there it meandered across the fields 'til it joined with other streams and became a small river running through the center of our valley.

"Less than half a day's ride on a slow horse, the hills and mountains rose on the far side of the valley. Our house was large and comfortable, considering where we lived. Father and Mother built it slowly and carefully over the years, adding rooms along the way 'til Mother had things just as she wanted them. It was painted white with dark green shutters and a veranda ran all along the front of the house. We often sat out there to shell peas, pit cherries, or snap beans and watch God paint glorious pictures of blazing crimson and gold in the sky at the end of the day.

"The kitchen was large with a comfortable pantry to one side. Our house was unusual because we had a front parlor with a fireplace where company could sit whilst visiting. Zella and I shared one attic room at the top of a very, very steep flight of stairs while Ralph slept in the other. Mother and Father had their bedroom next to the kitchen. To the south of our home, we had one of those great big, old-fashioned, red barns where the cows came every day to be milked and where the horses were stabled when the weather got too cold outside. We even had a few pig pens downhill and downwind of the house and a chicken coop where it was my job to gather the eggs. We had plenty o' milk and cream and we made our own butter. We also had plenty of . . . oh, there I go, getting off the subject."

Sarah stifled a small giggle. "You always do that, Grandma, but I don't mind."

Grandma Jenny chuckled and cleared her throat. "You are an angel, Sarah. Now where was I? Oh, yes.

"The day after Father hired Mr. Nie, Mother loaded two little red lard buckets full of extra food she had and sent me up the hill to deliver the food to the old folks. A rutted old woodcutting road wound its way up into the hills behind our house. The Nies had moved into the old sheepherder's cottage just where the hill topped out and the road crossed the creekbed. The road led right up to the door of their little black-sided shack, then turned right, crossed the stream, and continued on up into the hills.

"I wasn't too excited about trekking up that mountain road. You see, I was mighty afraid of snakes and just sure I'd see one on my way up to the little house. The Nies only lived half a mile up the road, it wasn't far to walk. But I'd seen a snake once on that rutted old dirt road and I could imagine the slithery little things just hiding in the chokecherry and mountain oak scrub bushes, waiting to jump out and get me. The sighing of a breeze through the quaking aspen leaves sounded slithery-like, and any little critter scurryin' through the tall grass made me jump and set my heart to racin'."

Grandma and Sarah both laughed at that because Grandma was still afraid of snakes.

"Thereafter, it was my duty ever' day to take two red buckets full of food to the Nie home. I never went once but what when I got to the top of the hill I could see the old man standing in the doorway watching for me.

"When I got there, he'd say, 'Come on in, girlie, while Mama unloads the little red buckets.' He always called Mrs. Nie 'Mama.' Mrs. Nie would unload things like potatoes, cornmeal, jams and jellies, a loaf of bread and some nice freshly made butter, milk and cream— just anything Mother had left over.

"Then Mrs. Nie would thank me and give me back the red buckets. I always walked discreetly to the edge of the hill, but once out of their sight, I kicked up my heels and I ran! With those buckets a-swingin' madly from the handles, I raced down that hill like those snakes were bitin' my heels."

"Grandma, Grandma," Sarah threw her arms around her Grandmother's neck and laughed while she hugged the surprised woman. "Instead of being Little Red Riding Hood taking a basket of goodies, you were Little Red Bucket–Hood. And instead of being chased by the Big Bad Wolf, you were chased by the . . . the . . . the Big Bad Snakes." Sarah laughed and laughed and Grandma hugged her sweet little granddaughter and laughed too.

When Sarah finally stopped laughing, she said, "Okay, Little Red Bucket–Hood, what happened next?" Grandma wiped a tear of laughter from her eyes and went on with the story.

The Small Wooden Box

 "As Christmas grew near and the weather outside turned blustery and cold, our house filled with warmth and wonderful smells. The wood fire in the parlor and the coal fire in Mother's kitchen stove both mixed with the smell of gingerbread, fruitcakes, fruit filled cookies, the pungent aroma of cinnamon mixed with sugar for the snickerdoodles, mincemeat and pumpkin pies, brandy pudding, and the homemade cinnamon hardtack candy—yum, yum, yum.

"Each year on December 23, Mother would get out all the red pails she had saved and fill them with the

special treats she always made at Christmas. Then early on the morning of Christmas Eve day, my whole family, all five of us, would squeeze into our little red and black sleigh behind Mick and Mort, our Belgian draft horse team, and ride around to the homes of our few neighbors. They were scattered all over the valley. It usually took us an hour of riding in that creaky old sleigh to get between houses. Father always put bells on the horse harnesses at Christmas time and they jangled cheerfully as the horses trotted across the snowy fields. The horses' breath billowed out in white clouds, forming icicles on their long chest hair. Ralph and Zella and I brought all our down-filled quilts and wool blankets and wrapped up tight with only our noses and eyes sticking out to watch the world go by. Even with all the blankets and quilts, we still froze, but it was fun anyway.

"At each house, our nearly frozen family would climb out of the sleigh and sing Christmas carols at the door of the home while our teeth chattered and our knees wobbled. *Jingle bells, jingle bells, jingle all the way* . . . (chatter, chatter, chatter) *We wish you a merry Christmas, we wish you a merry Christmas* . . . (shiver, shiver, shiver) *O tannenbaum, O tannenbaum* . . . By that time we could feel the blood flowing back into our feet and hands and the front door would be open. A cheerful family would pour out and welcome us to their home, wishing us a merry Christmas as well.

"Every family would invite us inside for a warm drink. It seemed like every house had a blazing fire and those yummy smells that come mostly at Christmas time. While the parents talked about grown-up stuff, we children would play around the Christmas tree, never too far from the fireplace.

"Most of the families had children who were either my age or the age of my sister Zella, who was thirteen. We all attended the same tiny one-room school house built in the center of the valley. My brother Ralph had a few friends as well, but they were all much older and spent their time talking about farm work and animals."

"That must have been crowded, everybody in one room," Sarah declared.

Grandma smiled. "Yes, sometimes there would be thirty children of all ages.

"Well, to get back to the story, Mother would always leave a little red bucket brimming over with Christmas treats for each family. Each of those buckets fairly reeked with cinnamon and ginger and cloves. And she often left with an armful of goodies from the family we had just visited. Every family seemed to have their own special Christmas treats that were always just a bit different from everyone else's. We looked forward to Mrs. Sorenson's snowy white divinity and rich chocolate fudge. Mrs. Burnett always made the most delectable pound cakes. If Zella hadn't watched me so closely, I'd have eaten every bit of those myself. Mrs. Vandewiele always sent us home with heavenly cinnamon rolls complete with pecans and raisins, just dripping with white creamy icing. Mrs. Kopp made the best cheese in the valley and at Christmas she always gave us four little round blocks of different types of cheese. Christmas and food, Sarah, they always seem to go together.

"This particular year that I'm telling you about was just a little different than the ones before. Ralph was the oldest child in our family. He had just turned nineteen in August of that year and he had his heart set on little Annie Mae Forrest. She was almost seventeen, petite with long blonde hair and blue eyes. Ralph was usually a very strong baritone singer, but I noticed that all of a sudden he seemed to have a real tough time getting any sound out when we got to the Forrest home. He looked down at his feet a lot and stumbled over the words. We were all cold, standing there in the December sunshine, so I rammed him in the ribs with my elbow in the middle of 'We Wish You a Merry Christmas.' He did a little better up through 'good tidings for Christmas,' then he just sorta faded out again.

"When the door opened, there stood pretty little Annie Mae, just a smilin' down on Ralph from their porch, battin' her long eyelashes and wearin' what I know was a new red Christmas dress. I took a peep sideways up at Ralph and saw a red color to match her dress creep up his neck and spread over his face. I knew he was a goner for sure. But thankfully, Annie Mae liked Ralph too, you could see it real clear. I looked at her, then I looked back up at Ralph. Even at nine years of age, I could see what was happening. When the Forrests invited us into their home, Zella and I went right on in with all of the parents. But as we went off to visit by the fire with their two younger girls, Ellen and Beth, I noticed that Ralph and Annie Mae stayed out on the porch. I didn't pay them any mind—if they wanted to stay out there and freeze, it was their own business. But they were still out there when Mother said it was time to be on our way, and they didn't look frozen to me."

"Grandma," Sarah interrupted, "was Ralph in love with Annie Mae?"

"Yes darling, he was very much in love with Annie Mae."

"Did Annie Mae love Ralph, Grandma?" Sarah asked.

"Annie Mae had loved Ralph from the time she was ten years old." Grandma rocked slowly back and forth as she talked. "I used to watch her sometimes when her mother brought Annie to our house. She was eight years older than me and seemed very beautiful and very grown-up. She had a musical voice when she talked and impish eyes when she laughed. I loved to watch her and wanted to be just like Annie when I grew up. When she smiled, her eyes would close real slow-like, then open up again and she seemed to look right out through her eyelashes. It was the prettiest thing. I loved to watch her smile. I tried to smile like Annie Mae, but I just couldn't get it right. And best of all, Annie was very kind to Zella and me. But if Ralph came around, I noticed that her eyes followed him wherever he was, whatever he was doing."

"So, did they get married, Grandma, and have lots of little children?" Sarah reached up and removed her Grandma's glasses and settled them carefully on her own little nose, peering out the window at the leafless trees bending back and forth in the wind.

"Wait a bit, angel, that's all part of the story."

"Okay, Grandma, keep going. I'll be patient," answered Sarah, leaning back again and squinting at the red buckets through Grandma Jenny's spectacles.

"It was almost full dark when we drove up the hill to sing carols to old Mr. and Mrs. Nie. It was late evening and theirs was the last house before we went home. We were all covered with our patchwork quilts and blankets, but I was just about frostbitten anyway and ready to curl up in front of our fire. It had been a long, fun-filled day and I was tired. I still remember the sleigh creaking, the bells jingling, and the horses snorting as we pulled up in front of their little dwelling. I peeked out of my blanket pile and noticed a small light shining forlornly through the one little window in their house. The leafless quakies and dark evergreen trees rose hauntingly behind the little house and scared me just a bit. I think the horses were impatient to be in their nice warm stalls in the barn, too, because Father had to tell them 'whoa' several times before they would stand still. Then old Mr. Nie opened the door and stepped outside. A thin shaft of light lit up the small porch and the snow on the ground. We children tumbled off of the sleigh and joined up in our chorus line, in a hurry to be done and on our way.

"*Jingle bells, jingle bells* . . . (chatter, chatter, chatter) I don't think our frozen voices were in tune, but we made up for that in volume.

"Old Mrs. Nie came out of the house and joined her husband. They stood there and listened to us sing. As the notes of the last carol rang out, Zella and I raced Ralph back to the sleigh, being pretty certain the Nies would not invite us into their home. But Mother, ever gracious and considerate, stepped forward with two little red buckets full of food and wishes for a merry Christmas. Father carried a third bucket, its brim overflowing with gingerbread cookies. Under those cookies were hidden two pairs of new socks, white ones for Mrs.

Nie, blue ones for her husband. Mother had knitted them herself.

"Wrapped once again in my thick old quilt, snuggled between Zella and Ralph, I watched from the sleigh and was a little embarrassed when I saw tears streaming down Mrs. Nie's face. She took two of the buckets and simply said 'Thank you.' Then she said, 'Wait.'

"She turned and hobbled quickly into the house. When she came out, she carried a box in her hand. Her eyes moved quickly to my father, then to my mother. She nodded with a tiny smile to each of them, but walked past to where I sat huddled in the sleigh. You could've knocked me over with a feather when she handed me the little box.

"In a voice choked with emotion, she said, 'My mum gave this to me. She's real special to me and I want you should have her. You'n' your red buckets have brung Christmas up the hill to us ever' day. Thank ya, Jenny.' "

"She gave you the box, Grandma?" asked Sarah, sitting forward again, looking over the spectacles and into her grandmother's eyes. "Why did she give you a present and nobody else got one?"

"Well, Sarah honey, I suppose she didn't have much of anything to give for presents."

"Oh, okay." Sarah paused and thought for a moment. "Go on, Grandma."

"Without another word, Mrs. Nie hugged me, turned and hugged my mother and my father, then she went to stand back on the porch with Mr. Nie. I saw her shivering in her thin dress and shawl as the cold night breeze whipped the material mercilessly. I didn't listen to much else that went on, but I do know my mother was crying real soft like when she got in the sleigh. She said something about them having so little, but willing to give so much. I didn't pay much attention at the time. I was too excited about getting the box.

"Once Mick and Mort were headed back down the hill, I had to protect my box from the grasping hands of Zella and Ralph. It was quite a tussle we had under all those blankets, but they didn't get my little box. They were very curious and just a little jealous. Soon we all just huddled together under our blankets, teeth chattering and arms and legs shaking. But beneath my blankets, I ran my hands over the sides of the little box, feeling and marveling at the intricate carvings. I barely noticed the rocking back and forth and the sleigh bells jingling as we headed home."

"But what was in the box, Grandma? Didn't you open it?" Sarah asked incredulously.

"No, I didn't want to open it while we were bouncing around in the sleigh. Besides, there wasn't any light in the sleigh and I was too cold. I wanted to wait for a special, quiet, *warm* time to look at my new treasure.

"Our family was gathered snugly and warmly around the Christmas tree later that evening as my father read from the book of Luke, 'And she brought forth her firstborn Son, and wrapped Him in swaddling clothes, and laid Him in a manger. And there were in the same country shepherds abiding in the field, keeping watch over their flocks by night.' "

"Grandma, do you have the whole Bible memorized?" asked Sarah.

"No, Sarah, my angel, just a few tiny pieces of it."

"Grandma, when did you open the box? What was in it?" Sarah begged, her fingers busy unclasping Grandma's imitation pearl necklace and trying to reclasp it around her own thin neck.

"Well, Sarah, I couldn't wait any longer either. So while Father finished reading the Christmas story, I climbed into my mother's lap and sat, just like you are right now, and carefully opened the little wooden box. The box was only yea high and so wide and maybe this long." Grandma waved her hands in the air to describe a box seven inches long, six inches wide and six inches high.

"I was so disappointed when I lifted the lid, because it looked as though the box was only filled with dingy, old, matted cotton. But Mother gently pinched the cotton between her fingers and carefully lifted it up. A layer of the drab cotton lifted cleanly out of the box." Grandma Jenny stopped rocking the chair and her small, weathered hands performed a dancing pantomime in the air, pretending to lift the cotton out of the box.

Bringing the imaginary box closer to Sarah's face, Grandma pretended to look inside and Sarah stared down into her grandmother's hands as though she, too, were looking into the box for the very first time.

"There inside, nestled among the matted cotton bed, was a very delicate, very beautiful figure of an angel. She was wrought from purest crystal and seemed to gather all the light in the room within her tiny form. Gently, I lifted her from the box. Her wings were wispy feathers of sparkling crystal, rising delicately on either side of her body as though fanning the heavenly air. Her glimmering dress swept back, then swirled around to her right side. When I turned the angel toward the firelight, her long hair seemed to billow and sparkle out behind her head as though it were being lifted by gentle breezes. Then the shimmering tresses fell in gentle folds, intermingling with the feathers of her wings. As I turned her back and forth, she caught and reflected a myriad of sparkling lights. Stunned with awe, I held the angel up to show my mother, only to find tears overflowing from her eyes.

"Father paused in his reading and turned to Matthew to read about the Wise Men. 'And when they were come into the house, they saw the young child with Mary his mother, and fell down, and worshiped him; and when they had opened their treasures, they presented unto him gifts: gold, and frankincense, and myrrh.'

"My mother's eyes were sparkling with tears and

her voice wavered a bit when she whispered, 'Jenny, this is a treasure both precious and rare. Mrs. Nie has given you her finest possession. Always cherish it, my little Jenny, and remember why she gave this to you.' "

Emily

 Grandma's hands dropped back down, one to hold Sarah, the other onto the arm of the rocking chair and she began again to rock slowly back and forth.

"Oh, Grandma, I could almost see her. She was beautiful! But why did she give the angel to you, Grandma? I don't understand," asked Sarah, her little brow furrowed in confusion.

"Sarah, let me ask you something. Have you ever been given a present that meant so much to you that saying 'thank you' just wasn't good enough?" Grandma looked seriously down at Sarah.

"Hmmm, let me think a minute." Sarah stared out the kitchen window for a moment or two, but everything was fuzzy, so she slid the glasses down her nose and peered impishly over their rims. "Nope, Grandma, I can't think of anything." Shrugging her shoulders, she lifted her little hands up to remove the black hair net from Grandma's hair. Wavy curls of silver hair intermingled with black fell below Grandma Jenny's ears and past the collar, just touching the back of her dress.

"Well, then you'll just have to imagine how you would feel if someone gave you something so wonderful that it made you all warm inside, something so marvelous that you just didn't have any words to say." Grandma paused for a bit. "Can you imagine that, Sarah?"

Sarah squeezed her eyes shut tight and leaned her head back for just a minute, then opened her bright blue eyes and nodded her little red head vigorously.

"Grandma, I know that if Daddy brings me a pony for Christmas, it will be so wonderful that I won't be able to say a word." Sarah had pulled the black hair net on, eyes wide, and was trying assiduously to tuck her bright red curls up into the net. "Does that count, Grandma, does it?"

"Yes, darling. That's how Mrs. Nie felt. I suppose having good food brought to her house every day made her feel so warm and wonderful inside that she didn't know what to say either. She had one precious possession and giving it to me and my family was the only way she could find to say thank you enough."

"Oh, okay, I understand now." Sarah leaned back and looked at the red buckets on the top shelf again. "Was that the end of the red buckets?"

"No, the red buckets were still there. Some days through the winter, Ralph would take me on his horse, Bo, up to the Nies' house so I wouldn't have to fight my way through the deep snow. Ralph was a great brother. He was the oldest, being ten years older than me. He seemed like a big hero in my eyes. He could do anything. He rode horses and roped cows. He farmed along with my father and helped my mother. Ralph always had a smile and kind word for anyone he chanced to meet. People just naturally loved Ralph. But he was busy most of the time helping with the running of the farm, so it was a very special treat to have him take me up behind him on his horse and ride up the hill. I would wrap my arms around his middle and hold on tight. He smelled of leather and pine, I distinctly remember. I s'pose it was because he always chopped wood for the house. I still love the smell of leather and pine.

"It was along about March when the spring winds start to blow to dry up all the snow and water that Mrs. Nie invited me to sit down and stay awhile. That was the first time she had ever asked me to stay. I have to admit, I was a bit nervous. But as I walked up the hill that day, the mud and slush from the melting snow had soaked through my boots and stockings and I was glad to get in out of the cold.

"As I took off my boots and hung my stockings by the fire to dry, Mrs. Nie told me I reminded her of the daughter she had once had. Her name was Emily. She had bright blue eyes and rich, curly dark brown hair that hung clear to her little waist. She liked butterflies and tulips best in all the world, Mrs. Nie told me. And her favorite color was yellow. But, as happened often in those days, Emily had caught rheumatic fever when she was just tiny and her heart was never well after that.

Mrs. Nie's beloved little daughter died just after she turned ten years old. Mrs. Nie showed me her only picture of Emily. It was a very old, very tiny, faded picture taken while Emily was still a baby. It hung in a locket around Mrs. Nie's fragile neck.

"It was such a sad story that I didn't know what to say, except that I was sorry. As soon as my stockings were dry, I put them back on, pulled on my boots, grabbed the handles of those little red buckets and headed for the door. I pulled the wooden latch and the door opened just a bit, then I stopped to look back at Mrs. Nie. She was just rocking slowly back and forth in front of the fire, her frail knees covered with an old, tattered quilt of faded colors. Then she turned her head and smiled at me, and thanked me for coming. Her smile lit the whole cabin up somehow, and my heart was lighter as I skipped and slid through the slush and mud back down the hill to my home.

"The next day, Mrs. Nie set out some of the sugar cookies Mother had sent the day before. Then she poured milk into two cracked cups, one for each of us. It was just like a grown-up tea party. The placemats she put on the table were pages from an old Montgomery

Ward catalog. The plates we ate from were chipped and didn't match, but it was special. Something she said made me laugh, and though I had always thought of her as "the poor old woman on the hill," that day my thinking changed. We chattered away for a long while and I discovered that she agreed with me that snakes were slithery, frightening, and not to be trusted. And she loved the little squirrels and rabbits of the forest and didn't think mean little boys should shoot their guns at them. She felt that big brothers were swell, while older sisters could be very irritating at times. She thought just the same way I did about so many things.

"When we had eaten the cookies and finished our milk, I properly rose to take my leave and she invited me to come back anytime. We both laughed, knowing I would be back the next afternoon. Then I put my coat on and ran all the way back down the hill. I felt I had made a new friend. When I got home I told my mother all about the tea party Mrs. Nie and I had enjoyed together.

"Mama told me that I could learn a lot from Mrs. Nie and that she was a remarkable individual. I thought that over, not sure just what Mother meant, then decided to think about it some other time. From then on, I looked forward to my daily visits to Mrs. Nie's house. She invited me to stay every day when I reached the top of her hill and we would have our little tea party. I had found a friend.

"During our next trip to the country store, Mother secretly bought a ten pound slab of chocolate and brought it home to surprise us. Chocolate was rare and expensive. The very next day Zella, Mother, and I made chocolate chip cookies. We made our own chocolate chips by chipping pieces of chocolate off of the big chocolate block. Needless to say, chocolate chip cookies were a very special treat for all of us.

"That afternoon, Mother carefully wrapped a dozen cookies in a tea towel and put them on top of the bread in one of the little red buckets for Mr. and Mrs. Nie, then handed the two buckets to me and kissed me goodbye.

"Ralph was just riding past the pole corral and up to the back porch when I stepped outside, a red bucket in each hand.

" 'Miss Jenny,' Ralph bowed low over the withers of his horse, cowboy hat in hand, 'would you and those

red buckets care to ride with me to Mrs. Nie's house?'
Ralph liked to pretend he was a fancy gentleman with a
deep southern drawl. His invitation was hilarious and
irresistible at the same time.

"I curtsied, laughing and trying not to spill the
buckets as I handed them up to him, then eagerly
climbed up behind his big leather saddle. We laughed
and talked all the way up the hill. Bo went slowly,
switching the newly hatched flies away with his tail.
He'd reach out and grab a mouthful of grass every little
ways and chew contently as he plodded up the road.
Ralph held my little red buckets, while I held onto him.
As Bo made his way up the hill, Ralph and I searched
for cloud shapes in the sky. I found an alligator that
turned into an eagle. Ralph found a turtle that turned
into four different fish, then quickly disappeared completely. It was a glorious day of bright sunshine and
vivid blue skies. A few hardy spring flowers were just
coming into bloomin' white, purple, and yellow
amongst the new green grass and budding trees beside
the road. Everything seemed right with the world.

"Mrs. Nie was pleased to see Ralph and invited
him to stay for tea. I lifted the tea towel full of cookies

out of the first bucket and showed her our special treat. We shared the chocolate chip cookies and fresh milk with Ralph and Mr. Nie, for after he saw the cookies, he decided to stay inside for the tea party that day. Then, when the cookie plate was empty, both men went back outside. As the door shut behind the menfolk, Mrs. Nie whispered to me that the only sure way to keep menfolk around was to feed 'em good food. 'Cause once that was gone, so were the men. We had a good laugh together, but we really started roaring as she pulled out four cookies that she had hidden away and saved just for us girls.

"It was that same day that I asked Mrs. Nie about the angel."

"Oh, Grandma, what did she say?" Sarah's eyes flashed with curiosity.

"She told me the crystal angel had been part of her family for three generations. Through each successive generation, the mother had given the angel to her daughter. When that daughter was grown into a woman, she gave the angel to her daughter, and down the line 'til it came to Mrs. Nie. The legend said that a guardian spirit followed the angel. But it wasn't 'til Mrs.

Nie's little daughter died that she felt the presence of the guardian spirit.

"She started by telling me a little about her mother and her grandmother, then she said, 'My mother gave me the angel when I was ten. She told me of the legend, that a guardian angel would be there to comfort me in times of sadness and to bring me happiness all through my life.'

"Mrs. Nie leaned forward in her rocking chair while she was talking to me and looked right in my eyes. Then she said, 'I thought the angel figurine was beautiful, but I didn't know if I believed the legend about the guardian angel. There were times when just looking at her, I would feel a sense of peace fill my heart and my troubles would float away for awhile. But I didn't discover my guardian angel until much later in my life. Then, three months after her tenth birthday, my sweet Emily got sick for the last time.'

"Mrs. Nie rocked back and forth in her chair, just staring at the ceiling for so long that I thought she had forgotten I was there. Feelings of sadness tugged at my heart for the pain I knew she was feeling. I looked around at the pitiful walls where the cold breezes snuck through cracks in the boards and tarpaper, at the barren earth floor which she swept each day and kept so tidy, at the single tiny glass pane in the side wall that let in a feeble amount of daylight, and it all made me want to cry. The pain in my chest was too great and I was just about ready to stand up and run out the door when she started in talkin' again.

" 'After my little Emily died, I was so awfully sad. It was as though the very heart of me had been crushed in my chest. When the casket was finally closed on her beautiful little face and curly brown hair—knowing her laughter would never again brighten my days—I truly wanted to die. I could eat no food, water stuck in my throat so I couldn't swallow. I was slowly slipping away when, several days after we buried Emily, I knelt beside her bed, begging God to tell me why my little girl had been taken away. I'm ashamed now to say that I was so furious with God that my prayer became one of great anger. Instead of asking for help, I turned on Him all my frustration and bitterness and pain at losing Emily! It wasn't long before my face was wet with tears of sorrow and anger. With trembling hands, I pulled open the drawer of Emily's nightstand to get out a handkerchief.

There, lying snugly among the scarves and handker-chiefs was the little crystal angel I had given to Emily only weeks before. She looked at me with that same sweet smile on her face, her shimmering arms begging me to pick her up.

" 'Ever so gently, I lifted her up and held her to the light from the window of Emily's bedroom. There seemed to be something different about her. Then a bright shaft of sunlight beamed through her and the most beautiful ethereal glow filled my hands and my heart as a heavenly light radiated through her and into me. In that instant, I changed my prayer to one of thanksgiving, for I had felt the presence of my guardian angel. Then, as now, I believed my guardian angel was my dear, sweet Emily, staying close to watch over me.' "

"Grandma, could you see the guardian angel too?" Sarah looked straight into her Grandmother's eyes.

"My heart was racing when I left Mrs. Nie's house that afternoon. I ran straight down the hill, in through the kitchen door, up the stairs to my bedroom, and directly to the wooden box on my dresser. I slid to a stop, then stood there taking great gulps of air, trying to catch my breath, keeping my eyes on that little box the whole time. When I could breathe a bit better, I said a little prayer, just a wee one. Then, slowly, with a trembling hand, I opened the box and took out the angel. I looked at her carefully, but nothing happened. She was beautiful and she gleamed, but she didn't glow. So I whirled around and quickly carried her to the window where I held her directly in the light shining through the glass panes. Still nothing."

"Does that mean you didn't have a guardian angel, Grandma?" Sarah's little shoulders slumped in disappointment. Her eyes were luminous with unshed tears, her auburn hair bundled in disarray beneath the black hair net and the dainty but oversized spectacles perched on her pert little nose. She looked so adorably sad that Grandma Jenny had to give Sarah a big hug.

"No, Sarah, I didn't have a guardian angel—then."

Ralph

"World War I, which began in 1914, was still being fought half a world away in Europe when I turned ten years old. Scraps of information about the Kaiser and the men who had gone to fight against him were traded by the men gathered at the livery stable and country store. Though I knew the rest of the world was engaged in a fierce battle for right and wrong, my happy young life had not been touched by the ugly realities of war. I lived in a beautiful, peaceful cocoon, insulated and safe, with no worries for the future. That bubble of serenity was forever shattered as the crocus flowers began poking

their blossoms out of the last snow, heralding the arrival of spring 1918, and Ralph announced that he was going off to fight in the great war. I remember so well his red hair and freckles and serious blue eyes as he announced his decision from the kitchen doorway.

"It was as though my mind just took a photograph of that moment. I can still see clearly the kettle steaming on the stove, bread was rising on the sideboard, I was washing the eggs I had just confiscated from the chickens, and Zella was churning cream into butter. Father had just about finished sharpening his favorite knife on the leather strop which hung by the back door and Mother's hands were deep in hot soapy dishwater. Then all movement ceased, as our eyes turned to Ralph. Mother started to cry, tears slowly welling in her eyes, running down her face and dropping into the soapy water. Father made one final swipe with his knife and split the leather strop cleanly in two. He stared numbly down at his hands, one holding a strip of burnished leather, the other a large knife. Finally, he raised his head and looked back at Ralph, though he didn't utter a sound for what seemed the longest time.

"Then the arguments erupted in a babble of confusion, with everyone talking at once. Father said Ralph couldn't go—how could he possibly run the farm by himself? Mother used emotions—what would Annie Mae say; did she want to wait two or three more years for Ralph? Zella and I looked at each other, seeing our own fear mirrored in the other's eyes. We didn't know what to say except, 'please don't go away.'

"Mother walked out to the barn with Ralph just before sundown and watched in silence as he saddled Bo and stepped up into the saddle. Zella and I watched from the window in our bedroom where we had gone to talk. Ralph leaned down and dropped a kiss on Mother's cheek, then he and Bo headed out through the front gate at a gentle lope. Mother turned and stood watching him go, her head high and her shoulders straight. We saw her hands come up to cover her mouth and we knew she was crying.

"Ralph rode west, towards Annie Mae's house, as the western sky erupted with incandescent gold and orange, amid strands of clouds painting a glorious sunset, even more vivid through our tears.

"When Ralph returned he didn't tell us what Annie Mae said. For the next two days, Mother and Father tried everything they could to change his mind. In the end, no arguments, no pleading, no amount of begging had any effect on Ralph. He loved his country and felt a strong desire to do his patriotic duty. So Mother helped him pack and the first of April we rode to the railroad depot and hugged and kissed Ralph for the last time. Zella's hazel eyes were puffy and streaked with red from holding tight to her emotions. I felt just dreadful, but I really wondered if my mother would live through the day. She, who was always so strong and capable, had one weak spot—that was my brother, Ralph.

"Ralph was standing on the bottom of the train steps, smiling and telling jokes, trying to cheer us all up. But his eyes frequently looked beyond our sad faces, searching, I knew, for Annie Mae. The conductor, all in black, blew his silver whistle and hollered, 'All aboard!' Suddenly Ralph's face lit up and he jumped down to the platform and ran along the dusty boardwalk.

"We all turned in time to see him sweep Annie Mae high off her dainty feet, hug her close and twirl her around in a circle. Before he set Annie Mae back on the ground, Ralph kissed her for the longest time. Then he set her gently back on her feet. Holding her hand in his, he led Annie Mae up to our family and announced that he and Annie planned to be married as soon as he returned. Her parents were there, nodding and smiling, sharing our happiness in their decision and sadness at Ralph's departure.

"We were so happy to know they were engaged that the sadness momentarily lifted. Then the conductor blew his whistle once more and the train slowly began its ponderous struggle to get underway.

"Ralph kissed Annie Mae once more, quickly hugged each of us, then turned as if to step onto the train. He surprised us by dashing to the edge of the platform where he jumped off and bent down quickly. He stood back up, two yellow daffodils in his hand. He raced back to where we stood and handed one each to Mother and Annie Mae. Then he raced to catch the train and he was gone.

"Amid our tears and sobs, the train wheels screeched and the iron beast puffed off, carrying its precious cargo east. We walked to the edge of the platform, waving hands and handkerchiefs. Mother and Annie Mae both clutched the yellow daffodils tightly to their bosoms. I walked to the edge of the platform and looked down. One more daffodil still bloomed there, just beside the steps leading up to the dusty, wooden train platform. As tears filled my eyes, I turned away from the departing train and looked at the bright, yellow flower. I remember, strangely, blocking out Ralph's departure and wondering how those daffodils could possibly have grown there beside the dilapidated old platform where the smoke and dust of countless trains constantly assailed its delicate petals. Then I could no longer see it clearly, for the tears in my eyes blurred its jovial color. The lonesome wail from the locomotive whistle echoed back with the rolling puffs of black smoke as I turned to follow my family back to our wagon. We all hugged Annie Mae, then she rode away with her parents and we headed home.

"We received several letters from Ralph before he left the United States. Mother lived for those letters. When Ralph went into the army, they gave him the standard haircut. He rescued one beautiful curly red lock and sent it to my mother. I think he also sent one to Annie Mae. Mother carefully wrapped the precious red curl in white tissue paper and locked it away with all her life's treasures in the jewelry box in her room. From then on, we made regular appearances at the post office.

"Mother was giving me a lesson in making bread early one Saturday morning when Mr. Maeser, the storekeeper, rode up on his old gray gelding. He tied his horse to the hitching rack in front of the house and knocked on our door. While Mother cleaned the flour off of her hands, I raced to the front door, sticky hands and all. I welcomed him into our home and asked him to sit down. He was carrying a package wrapped in brown paper. That alone set my heart to racing. We seldom received packages and I was very curious to know what was in it. Mother came into the parlor, wiping her hands on a towel. Mr. Maeser explained to her that this package had arrived from Ralph, addressed to her, and he had another errand out this way, so he had brought it along.

"Mother sent me to get Mr. Maeser a glass of water while she began to unwrap the package. I raced to the kitchen, pumped and pumped 'til the water came through the kitchen faucet and I had a glass full of water. Then I ran back to the parlor, slopping water over the edge of the glass all the way. I handed the wet glass to Mr. Maeser, but barely heard his kind 'thank you' because my attention was centered on the box Mother was trying to open.

"The box was open now and Mother gently withdrew a foot-long, oval, wooden picture frame. Protected by the curved glass front was a wonderful picture of Ralph dressed in his new army uniform. He looked very official in his smart uniform, hat cocked off to the side, and his hair cut short. He wasn't smiling, so he looked very serious, but it was Ralph, all right. Mother's face lit up with a glorious smile and she brushed tears from her eyes with the back of her hand.

" 'Thank you for bringing this to me, Mr. Maeser.' Mother looked up at him. 'Would you care to stay for dinner, we're going to be having stew and corn bread in just a little while?'

" 'No, thank you. I have a couple more stops to make, then I'm going to stay at my sister's house and head back to the store in the morning. They're expecting me for dinner, so I'd better not disappoint them. Glad you enjoyed your package.' He strode to the door as he spoke to Mother, then he was on his horse and riding away.

"Mother gave me a quick hug and told me to run out to the shed and find a hammer and a nail, for she intended to hang Ralph's picture right now. So, off I went. I found my father in the shed and told him about the package, so he reached for his hammer, then found a nail. Hand in hand, we ran together back to the house. By the time we huffed and puffed into the parlor, Mother was holding Ralph's picture up where she wanted it to hang. Several minutes later, Father had pounded the nail into the wall and there hung Ralph's likeness in the center of the wall directly above the fireplace. He looked good there. Then we all sat close to each other on the sofa while Mother read the letter Ralph had sent with the picture.

"Ralph and some of his friends, wearing their new uniforms during a trip to town, had come across a photographer's shop. After a short discussion, all but one of their group went into the shop and had their portraits taken. Ralph was being shipped out to France before his picture would be developed, so he had purchased the oval frame and left enough money for the photographer to ship the completed portrait to his family. He told us how anxious he and his new friends were to be off to fight in the war. He sent his love and promised to write as soon as he reached Europe.

"Later, Father went back out to finish what he had been working on and Mother and I went back to the bread. The dough had raised in the bowl, so we carefully divided it up, moved the pieces to a flat pan, and cooked it that way. It was the most strangely shaped bread I ever remember eating, but it wasn't too bad. For years afterward, whenever we looked at the picture of Ralph above the fireplace, we thought of those lumpy, flat loaves from the first time I made bread.

"Ralph sent us one hilarious letter when he reached France. He described all of the people and his attempts to communicate. He said there were no girls as cute as his little sisters. No one could cook like his beloved Mother. He told us how tasteless the eggs were and how skinny the cows looked. He said the farmers could take a few lessons from his father. Then he wrote that it looked like the war would end soon and he should be home before we knew it. His commander had promised Ralph he would be home by Christmas.

"Mother started counting the days till Christmas,

and I ran all the way up the hill to tell Mrs. Nie that Ralph would be home for Christmas."

"Oh, Grandma, I was so afraid he would die. I'm glad he came home." Sarah sighed in relief.

"Wait, sweetheart."

Tragedy

"Zella, who had just turned four-teen, and I were sitting high on a haystack one August day when a truck drove up our road. Any motorized vehicle driving up our road was a most unusual circumstance and it immedi-ately drew our attention. Dust billowed up and swirled around the truck as it rolled to a stop. When the dust settled, a man in uniform got out and walked into the alfalfa field to speak with my father. The man in uni-form handed our father a yellow envelope. Father stood very still for the longest time, then he walked slowly with the man back to his truck. He shook the man's

hand and as the truck rumbled away, Father walked with dragging steps up to the house. He paused on the top step and leaned for a moment on the veranda support post, his head bowed on his chest. Then he shuffled slowly forward and the screen door slammed behind him. We heard our mother scream, then everything went silent; no birds chirped, no cows mooed. It was as if the world stopped for that moment.

"Ralph was dead. He died of spinal meningitis June 25, 1918, in France. Mother was devastated. We all felt his loss keenly, but she took his death harder than the rest of us. The army sent Ralph home to us in a sealed casket. We buried him in the family plot beside Mother and Father's only other son, a child who had died before he was two years old.

"Annie Mae Forrest and her family came to the funeral as well as all of our neighbors across the valley. Zella and I stood by Annie Mae and hugged her while we all cried. We didn't know what else to do. We all held a flower to drop onto Ralph's casket. I had picked a mountain bluebell, Zella a yellow and white daisy. But when Annie Mae walked past the casket, she tearfully laid down a dried and faded yellow daffodil. A week later, Annie Mae left to go to a boarding school back east. She never returned to our valley.

"Throughout that summer and fall I'd see Mother baking bread or shelling peas, or just doin' any of a hundred different tasks. Her hands would slowly fall silent and still, a faraway look in her eyes. Then I knew she was thinking of Ralph.

"I was just coming out of the chicken coop with my bucket full of eggs one morning when I heard Mother crying softly somewhere nearby. I set down the bucket of eggs, then went to find her. She was standing beside the wooden box Ralph had built, when he was just a boy, that now held curry combs, brushes, and halters for the horses. Her hand was brushing gently back and forth across the letter 'R' which Ralph had so carefully carved into the lid. I walked up and just wrapped my arms around her. I felt Zella's arms reaching from the other side and enveloping both of us. Then from out of nowhere, Father was there, wrapping his arms around all of us. Ralph was gone. We would always miss him, but we still had each other."

Grandma Jenny stopped speaking for several moments. The rocking chair creaked back and forth several more times, then she cleared her throat, scooted Sarah off her lap and stood up.

"Grandma, that's not the end of the story, is it?" Sarah's voice trembled and her blue eyes filled with tears.

"No, sweetheart, I just need to put the loaves into the oven or they will be flat and we'll have pancakes instead of bread." Grandma lifted the towel off three smooth, round, white loaves of bread and one little loaf brimming over with personality. She opened the oven door and gently slid each loaf onto the middle rack. Then she gently shut the door.

The Present

I told Mrs. Nie all about Ralph, shared with her all my memories of him. She knew how it helped me to talk. I told her how his red hair would shine in the sunshine and look like fire sometimes, and how his blue eyes would flash in anger or twinkle with humor. I cried when I told her how much we loved him and missed him. Mrs. Nie knew so very well the pain I was going through. She had lost much in her life and she truly understood.

"After a time, our little tea parties once again resumed their laughter and talk of lighter subjects: the latest fashions in the Montgomery Ward catalog, the

other children at school, chores I didn't like to do. Mrs. Nie was the nicest lady and I really enjoyed going to see her every day. I know she was an old woman and I was a young girl, but we became best friends. I could tell her anything and soon I knew, without a doubt, that she loved me. Pretty soon I wasn't even afraid of the snakes anymore."

"That's amazing, Grandma," laughed Sarah, wiping the final tears from her eyes. "Then why did you jump when that water snake slithered out from under the porch this morning?"

Grandma chuckled. "Well, not as afraid as I was before, how's that?

"Well, somewhere around the middle of October, Mrs. Nie caught a real bad cold. She was laid up in bed for a couple of weeks. During that time I didn't get to take the little red buckets full of food up to her house. Instead, my mother would go up there a couple of times a day with medicine and all sorts of things to try to get Mrs. Nie better. We had no antibiotics back then or electric blankets or even hot showers or baths in which to soak. When you got sick in 1918, you just climbed under a stack of blankets, drank gallons of chicken soup, and suffered 'til you got better. There was no doctor in our valley so my mother did all the doctorin'. Mother was known all over the valley for her medicinal skills. If someone was sick, or having a baby, or broke a leg or an arm, they came hot-foot to get my mama. My father said she was just a natural born healer.

"I could tell Mother was real worried about Mrs. Nie because she didn't let me go see her for such a long time. I missed her badly. I had other friends, but none quite so special as Mrs. Nie. I remember it was on a Sunday afternoon following Bible reading in our front parlor that Mama told me I could start taking the little red buckets back up to Mrs. Nie the next afternoon. I was ecstatic!

"When I got home from school, Mother had the buckets waiting for me on the kitchen table, heaped and brimming over with food. I just took time to drop my books, grab those little red buckets, and I was out the door and almost to the barn before I heard it slam shut behind me. I never made the trip up that hill so fast.

"Old Mr. Nie was standing at the door, just like he always was before. 'Come on in, girlie, while Mama unloads the little red buckets.' He always said the same thing.

"I went on in and lifted the buckets onto the old table. I glanced quickly at Mrs. Nie, then quietly unloaded the food onto her table. Amongst the other items, Mother had sent a mason jar full of chicken broth. I reached for a cup and poured some of the still-warm soup into it, then carried it carefully across the small room and placed it in Mrs. Nie's frail hand. I was rewarded with a tired, but grateful smile. Then I pulled a chair close to the fireplace and sat down facing Mrs. Nie.

"The weather was getting colder now, so late in the fall. Mrs. Nie sat in her rocking chair, all wrapped up in blankets and old quilts, looking so drawn and pale that I began to worry. Her hands looked like withered claws as they carefully held the cup to her lips and she sipped the warm broth. She drank it all while we watched the flames dance in the hearth in silence for a few moments. I breathed a heart-felt sigh of relief when she finally broke the silence and asked me how my day at school had gone and what had happened in the weeks I'd been away. I just gushed out everything as fast as my tongue could race. When I had run out of news to share, we both sat quietly once again and watched the fire consume the wood in the stone hearth.

" 'Your mama is a wonderful woman, Jenny,' she said. 'I've never known no better. Kinder, sweeter folks than yours just can't be found.'

"I didn't know what to say. I knew my mother and father were good people. I suppose I just sorta took it for granted. They were what they were and always had been.

" 'I feel real terrible about that brother of yours, Ralph. His dying way over there on the other side of the world sure has caused your mama a lot of grief. But with that horrible war going on over there, I s'pose there's bound to be lots of mamas with broken hearts.' She started coughing something awful and it stopped her from talking anymore.

"Mrs. Nie coughed a lot after that. But in between her coughing spells, we still talked a lot and we decided we'd make my mother a wonderful Christmas present. We had time if we worked real hard every afternoon when I brought up the red buckets. She called her husband in and we discussed our idea with him and he eagerly agreed to help. I never got to know Mr. Nie very well, I'm sad to say, but he was always kind and gentle-spoken and willing to help. My feet fairly flew down the hill that night. I don't think they ever touched the ground from her doorstep to mine.

"Mama could tell something was up because, while I set the table for dinner that night, she asked me what mischief I was brewing."

"Well, Grandma, what mischief were you brewing?" asked Sarah.

"Oh, that's coming, darling. Now where was I? Oh yes. After that, every day I would stay up at Mrs. Nie's as if we were having our tea party. But instead, we worked on Mother's Christmas present. Some days Mrs. Nie's cough seemed to be less painful than others. But I could tell the coughing made her dreadfully tired most of the time and I worried about her. Even though Mrs. Nie was sick, she worked hard with Mr. Nie and me to finish the Christmas present on time."

"Grandma, what was it?" Sarah grabbed her arm and shook it hard. "You have to tell me." Her little voice was plaintive and pleading.

"Wait, angel. Just wait. The snow started falling that year right on Thanksgiving Day and it didn't let up. My father let me ride Ralph's horse up to Mrs. Nie's house the whole last week before Christmas, the snow was so deep. He said Bo was my horse now. That helped too, somehow, to sit in Ralph's saddle and pet old Bo's neck and talk to him on the way up the hill. I talked to him of Ralph once in awhile and he would flick his ears attentively back and forth. Sometimes, I swear he knew what I was talking about for he would let out a little nicker from time to time.

"We worked hard, and I was so afraid we wouldn't have the present done on time. But three days before Christmas, our present was finished and the three of us sat contentedly around Mrs. Nie's table and admired our handiwork.

"Mr. Nie reached out his gnarly, workworn hand and lovingly took Mrs. Nie's in his. I watched them share a tender look, then Mr. Nie simply said, 'Mama— it'll do.'

"Mr. Nie never did say very much, but I knew he loved his wife. One corner of his mouth turned up in a little smile and he said, 'Well, I got chores to do.'

"With that, he stood up and was out the door leaving me alone with Mrs. Nie and the present. We decided we'd save the present and surprise Mother on the night when my family went around caroling to all the valley families, Christmas Eve. I was simply bursting with anticipation of the great surprise we had in store. It was difficult, but I kept our secret."

The Storm

 "I lay awake staring sightlessly into the darkness surrounding me while the wind moaned around the house all night before Christmas Eve day. I couldn't sleep, tossing and turning on my feather mattress, shifting and pulling the covers 'til I was hopelessly tangled up. I forced myself to lie perfectly still when the shutters banged against my window, the echo booming through our small attic room. The sounds of wind and swirling snow that night seemed extra sad, somehow.

"I hopped out of bed as soon as I heard Father stirring downstairs, grabbed my clothes and scrambled

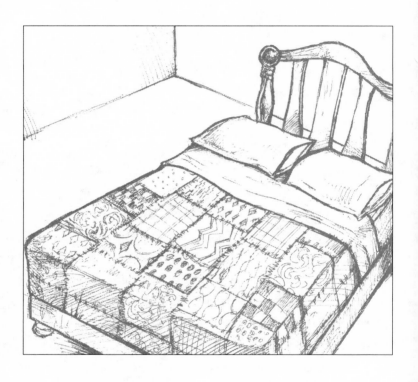

right back under the covers to dress. Zella and I shared one bed in the quaint little room at the top of our house. I don't know how, but Zella had slept all night, occasionally mumbling in her sleep. So, as I headed down the steep stairs to the kitchen, I shook her shoulder—a bit roughly, I must admit—and told her to wake up. I was ornery enough that if I couldn't sleep, well then, neither should she.

"By the time I got downstairs, my father had a fire blazing away in the kitchen stove. The heat was marvelous and I stood just as close to the stove as I could without burning myself. Ooh, but it was a cold morning.

"Father stomped his feet into his tall work boots and buttoned his heavy sheepskin coat securely in place. Using a long red, knitted scarf, he tied his fur hat tightly to his head, then pulled on his warmest gloves. After getting completely protected from the cold, Father bravely opened the door and headed out into the storm to milk the cows. A fierce wind blew snow and bits of ice through the door and whirled it around the kitchen. It felt like all the heat was instantly gone. Then he was outside and the door slammed shut behind him.

"I started getting breakfast ready. I knew when he got back from his early morning chores today, Father would be especially hungry. My mother came out of her room just a moment later and gave me a warm hug. Zella came sleepily down the stairs and helped set the table. Breakfast was just about ready and the table was set when 'Bang!' the door burst open and crashed back against the wall.

"My father burst into the room in a cloud of blowing snow, then slammed the door shut behind him. He carried a large milk can in each hand and a bucket of eggs hung from his neck. He set down the milk cans and, with a big smile, handed me the bucket of eggs. Then he shook great flakes of snow from his hat, coat, and gloves onto the floor where little pools of water formed. When he had his outer clothing off and hung up on pegs, we all sat down to breakfast.

" 'How does it look outside?' My mother had waited 'til we were all eating before she asked.

" 'We probably got a good two feet of snow just last night, Charlotte. The wind has blown some drifts as high as the first floor of the house and to the eves of the barn.' He paused to take a bite of fried potatoes, then chewed quietly for a moment.

"'I had to break trail all the way to the barn. Then I had to tunnel my way through a four-foot wall of drifted snow just to get to the barn door. But the animals are fine. I milked the cows and gathered the eggs.' Here he winked over at me. 'I don't want my girls out there in that snowstorm. I also strung a rope from the barn door to our back door so we can find our way across the yard easier. That wind and snow make it darned near impossible to see where you're going outside. After breakfast, I'll see if I can get down to the pig pens and see how the sows are makin' out.' He attacked his plate of food again.

"Suddenly I felt a cold chill creep into the pit of my stomach. 'Father,' I asked, 'will we still be able to go caroling tonight?'

"His hand, with a fork full of sausage, stopped halfway to his mouth. 'No, pumpkin, I don't think we're going anywhere until this storm lets up. Once the wind stops, it will probably take us several days just to dig out.' Then he chuckled and added, 'We'll just have a quiet day here in the house and sing to ourselves tonight.'

" 'Mother,' I cried, 'how will I get the food buckets up to Mrs. Nie today?' Actually, I was thinking of the present. How was I going to get our present down here to give to Mother tomorrow for Christmas?

" 'Jenny, I'm sure Mr. and Mrs. Nie will be quite all right for a few days. I'm sure she has saved some of the food from time to time and will have enough to winter over for a short time. There's no need to worry,' she reassured me.

"Mother could probably see the anxiety in my face, but of course she didn't know the full extent of my concern.

"I stewed and fretted all day. Every little while I would go to the window, pull the cream-colored drapes aside and look out to see if the snow had quit falling. But it just got worse and worse. I tried to darn socks with Mother. I tried to play games with Zella. I wrote in my diary. Nothing helped. It was the longest day of my life!

"Darkness settled over the snow falling outside and Father went out to tend to the animals again while

Mother and Zella and I fixed dinner. Zella was very impatient with me. 'You're acting like a caged animal, Jenny,' she complained in her sharp voice. 'You should enjoy a day off from all the chores! Be grateful you have a nice home to live in so you don't have to be out in the cold and snow, silly girl.' "

A Visitor

"It was later that evening, as we all gathered snugly in front of our fire, that Father pulled out the old Bible once more and opened to the book of Luke. I studied the homemade ornaments on our Christmas tree. There were the usual strings of popped corn and cranberries. Gracing the end of many of the tree's limbs were the finger-length white candles Zella and I hand-dipped just the week before. Getting them to stand up straight on the tree was a talent only Mother possessed. Red pieces of snipped tin, of varying shapes and sizes, hung throughout the branches of the

evergreen tree. These had been formed using tin snips and cutting up several of the little red buckets over the years. Stars, circles, and squares—one side of each bright red, the other shiny silver—were suspended on red yarn. Hanging free, they twirled and danced in the air currents, giving the whole tree a glittering effect.

"My eyes were drawn lovingly to the nine wooden stars, nestled carefully amongst the green pine needles. Ralph had carved one every Christmas after he turned ten. Almost hidden amongst the other decorations were two lopsided angels Zella and I had crocheted last Christmas. Seeing them reminded me of last year and how I had first held the little wooden box with the beautiful crystal angel given to me by Mrs. Nie. So much had happened in one short year.

"This night the little angel sat atop her wooden box on the mantle above the fireplace. As I looked up at her and watched slivers of light glisten from the tips of her wings, I felt tears burning the back of my eyes. I just stared at the fire so no one could see how I felt. A vise was squeezing my heart deep in my chest and I had to breath out of my mouth so I wouldn't make any sobbing sounds. I knew we could give Mother our present after the snowstorm cleared, but somehow it just wouldn't be the same.

"Father had just turned back to read about the Wise Men, 'Now when Jesus was born in Bethlehem of Judaea in the days of Herod the king . . .' when suddenly there was a loud knock on the kitchen door.

"We all jumped, then turned our astonished faces toward each other. Surely no one could be knocking at our door in the middle of a ferocious snow storm. Then suddenly it was there again. Bang, bang, bang!

"We all lunged to our feet and rushed into the kitchen. Zella reached the door first and threw it open wide. A ghostly, snow-covered figure shuffled through the door. The door slammed shut again and the storm was locked back outside. Snow fell to the floor as the tattered hood was thrown back revealing the smiling face of Mrs. Nie. We were so shocked, no one could say a word. She had never been down to our house, even when the weather was good. But for her to make the trek on such a night as this . . . Well, it was astounding.

"Mother finally stepped forward. 'My dear Mrs. Nie,' she said, 'please come in by the fire. Take your coat off and tell us how you got here. We're so glad you came . . . it's such a pleasure to have company on Christmas Eve . . . but with this awful storm . . . and . . . and how is your cough?'

"As she helped Mrs. Nie take off her coat and gloves, I saw Mother trade an astonished look with my father. Then we were all tromping back into the living room. I walked right up next to Mrs. Nie and wrapped my arms around her slender waist, hugging her tight. There wasn't anyone I wanted to see more tonight and I saw right off that she was carrying a large bundle. My heart leaped in my chest, I was so happy and excited.

"As she hobbled through the arched doorway from the kitchen into the parlor, Mrs. Nie saw the open Bible laying where Father had been sitting. 'Oh, were you reading the Christmas story?' she asked.

" 'Why, aaah, yes, we had just finished when we heard your knock at the door.' My father was clearly still in shock.

" 'Would you mind terribly, I mean, if it wouldn't be too much trouble . . . could you read it again, for me? I haven't heard it in such a long time.' Her eyes glistened a little, and I couldn't tell if it was from the firelight or if she had tears in her eyes.

" 'I'd be honored,' my father said and we all sat back down. Mother gave Mrs. Nie her comfortable rocking chair, and perched herself beside Father. I couldn't take my eyes off the bundle Mrs. Nie held in her lap as I curled up on the floor at her feet.

" 'And it came to pass in those days that there went out a decree from Caesar Augustus, that all the world should be taxed.' My young and impatient spirit shut out my father's voice at first. With my eyes fixed on the bundle in Mrs. Nie's lap, I recalled the expressions on her and her husband's faces as we sat at their table three days before with the completed present. Then my father's voice became clear in my mind, '. . . and, lo, the angel of the Lord came upon them, and the glory of the Lord shone round about them: and they were sore afraid.

" 'And the angel said unto them, Fear not: for, behold, I bring you good tidings of great joy, which shall be to all people.' "

A certain quality had come into my father's voice as he read, " 'Ye shall find the babe wrapped in swaddling clothes, lying in a manger.

" 'And suddenly there was with the angel a multitude of the heavenly host praising God and saying,

Glory to God in the highest and on earth peace, good will toward men.'

Each word seemed to fill my heart fuller and fuller, 'til I thought I could hear no more. My eyes moved slowly from the bundle to Mrs. Nie, to my mother, to Zella, to my father, to the angel on the mantle. Slowly and deliberately my father read the final words, " 'And when they had opened their treasures, they presented unto him gifts; gold, and frankincense, and myrrh.' "

Guardians

"Never had the Christmas story touched my heart with such force. I looked around again at my sister and mother and father and I could tell it had touched them deeply as well. I looked into Mrs. Nie's eyes and saw a glow of such love and happiness that my heart nearly overflowed within me. Her gentle smile touched me and each of the others in turn, then her eyes lowered to the bundle resting so mysteriously in her lap.

"I watched as her workworn hands gently unfolded the material she had wrapped around the bundle. The

last layer of material came off and there it was for all to see. But it was so much more beautiful than I had remembered, that I clapped both hands over my mouth and the breath caught in my throat. I watched in amazement as Mrs. Nie carefully placed our gift in my mother's hands.

" 'Merry Christmas, Charlotte, from Mr. Nie, and Jenny and me.'

"It was a chest fashioned of finest cedar. With exquisite care, Mr. Nie had carved an oval frame into each panel of the chest. Within each oval frame were two little red buckets, one bucket standing, the other laying on its side. They were painted the same color red as the little lard buckets Mother filled and I carried to Mrs. Nie's house each day. Golden mountain oak leaves were carved beneath the oval frame, adding gracefully curving lines to the beauty of the box. Each corner of the lid and the bottom of the box was protected by brass corner brackets, molded to fit the wood and carefully nailed in place. The elegance of Mr. Nie's skill and craftsmanship was evident in every line of the box.

"As tears filled my mother's eyes, Mrs. Nie spoke gently, her voice filled with love and compassion.

" 'This is your hope chest, Charlotte. Mr. Nie carved the buckets into the sides of the chest and Jenny painted them. They are to always remind you of the many little red buckets that your family has filled and sent up the hill to us. Your love and kindness and generosity meant even more to us than the food. They gave us the faith that we could survive here and they gave us hope that the future could be even better than the past.'

" 'We wanted to give something back to you. With all my heart, I want this small hope chest to return to you even a small part of the hope and faith you have given to us.'

"The fire crackled quietly in the hearth. Mother held the wooden chest in her lap and gently ran her finger over the etched wood. A tender smile curved her lips and teardrops filled her eyes and slowly rolled down her cheeks.

"She finally opened the lid. It lifted silently on shiny brass hinges to reveal a deep red velvet lining. The sweet fragrance of cedar filled the Christmas air. Nestled securely in the red velvet was a crystal figurine—which I had not yet seen.

"Tears were now streaming freely down Mother's face so that I don't know how she could see. She reached carefully into the wooden chest and brought out a glittering angel. She held it up with both hands so that the firelight sparkled in and around it. Her hands seemed to glow from the radiance of the angel. I glanced swiftly at my angel standing silently on the mantle, her wings shining dimly in the reflected light above the fireplace.

"When I looked back, I saw Mrs. Nie touch Mother on the shoulder. Mother turned, a radiant and hopeful look on her face. Mrs. Nie stared deeply into my mother's eyes. Her voice was quiet, but her sweet tones carried throughout the room.

" 'Ralph is happy and well, Charlotte. I came to tell you so you won't worry about him anymore. Accept this small gift from me, for you have been my angel. God bless you.'

"Mother looked into Mrs. Nie's eyes for another moment, then a tiny smile of joy lifted the corners of her mouth. She looked back down at the buckets carved into the side of the hope chest and then again at the angel. She couldn't speak. None of us could. We were all staring at the shimmering figurine, Mrs. Nie's words about Ralph ringing in our ears.

"Mother handed the angel to my father. As he held it up to the firelight, I saw tears welling over the edges of his eyes and making twin trails down his cheeks. Zella held it next and I watched as her lower lip trembled and tears flowed from her eyes. Then it was my turn.

"I knew why they cried. Whereas my angel was fragile and ethereal, this angel radiated strength and vitality. It was the figure of a young man with short, windswept hair. He was clothed in a long robe, his feet barely visible beneath the glittering folds of crystal material. Powerful wings swept straight back, lifting high in a peak above his head. His strong arms seemed to be reaching for me. When I lifted him up and turned him to catch the light from the fire, I cried out softly in amazement. Mother, Father, and Zella all leaned closer to see what had caused my outburst.

"For an instant, as the light from the fire touched his head, his hair took on a red glow and I was sure I saw a sparkle of blue in his eyes. A cry escaped my mother's lips. I believe she saw the same thing, though we never spoke of it after that. Mother's eyes were wide and luminous as she turned, in surprise and awe, to ask

Mrs. Nie about this angel. We all turned, unformed questions tumbling over in our minds.

"But Mrs. Nie wasn't there. The fire spluttered and crackled as we looked at each other in silence, and the chair where Mrs. Nie had been sitting rocked slowly back and forth. Then we all heard the kitchen door closing.

"I jumped up with a cry and whirled around. 'Why did she go?'

"Father, Zella, and I ran quickly to the kitchen door to call Mrs. Nie back into the house. The storm outside was still ferocious. But Mrs. Nie was not there. She was gone as mysteriously as she had come. Her tracks led off in the snow along the line Father had tied from our back door to the barn. Already the blowing snow was filling in the tracks. Father didn't hesitate. He ran out of the house, holding tight to the rope and disappeared into the howling, blowing snow. Mother came and the three of us stood in the door 'til we were almost numb, calling her name, listening to the howling wind, waiting for our father to return.

"We all let out a sigh of relief when Father reappeared through the blowing snow. But he was alone.

Though the wind tried to blow him off course, he held tight to the lifeline that was guiding him back to his family. We all hugged him when he reached the door, then drew him into the kitchen and shut the door on the cold and storm.

" 'I couldn't find her. She was just gone,' Father panted in a perplexed tone of voice.

"We were quiet as we walked together back into the front parlor. I still had the boy angel in my hands, having forgotten about him in our worry over Mrs. Nie. But as I lifted him up and looked at him again, sparkling in the light of the fire, an indescribably warm feeling of peace started way down in my stomach and seemed to race right up through my chest and into my mind. Somehow, I knew in that moment that Mrs. Nie was all right.

"I walked over to where my mother was sitting once again in her rocking chair and gently handed her the angel. As I looked into her eyes I could see that the pain, which had etched her face since Ralph's death, was gone. Zella came over and linked her arm in mine as we watched Mother turn the angel back and forth.

" 'Ralph really is okay, I know that now,' Mother

whispered peacefully as the fire sparkled on the angel and warmed the buckets carved into the front of the hope chest. Then, in a voice I could barely hear, 'Thank you Mrs. Nie; your gift is gratefully received.'

"I went to the mantle above the fireplace and gently lifted down the angel Mrs. Nie had given to me. As I held her up to the firelight, I saw and felt her glow, from the firelight, through the angel, and into my heart. I knew then that I had a guardian angel, just as Mother now had one. And I thought I knew who it was.

"A chill ran down my spine as I remembered the words Father had read just moments before, 'and they had opened their treasures . . . gold, and frankincense, and myrrh.' "

Hope

"Three days later the storm blew itself out and the next day Father hooked the team up to the plow and started clearing roads. It took him most of that day to get a path plowed through the drifts all the way up the hill. I packed two little buckets with the best food we had in the pantry, then we all jumped into the sleigh, carrying blankets and bundled against the bright, cold evening. The sun had risen in a clear blue sky, and was now lowering in a brilliant scarlet sunset as we reached the Nie home.

"We all scrambled out of the sleigh and formed up

in our chorus line, Mother and Father behind, Zella and me in the front. We began our carols with 'Joy to the World.' It was the most beautiful chorus we had ever performed. The final phrase of the song still resounded in the clear air as the door slowly opened and Mr. Nie hobbled out onto the porch. He looked haggard and drawn, his steps slow and faltering. Mother and Father rushed to him to ask what was wrong. He looked as though he hadn't shaved or combed his hair in days and it looked like he had slept in his clothes. We all gathered close to listen.

"It was then that we learned how ill Mrs. Nie had been when the storm started, how she had quickly weakened. With a shaking voice, Mr. Nie told how she had smiled at him before she died, told him how much she loved him, and promised to return when it was his time to come to the other side. Then she had closed her eyes and she was gone.

" 'Oh, no,' my mother cried in anguish, 'I knew she shouldn't have come to our home during the storm Christmas Eve.' Then she sagged against my father's shoulder and started to sob.

" 'Mama couldn't have, Mrs. Perry.' Mr. Nie had a

strange look on his face as he gazed around at each of us. 'She couldn't have come to your house Christmas Eve because she . . .' his voice wavered and he paused to swallow a couple of times, 'it . . . it couldn't have been Christmas Eve . . . because . . . because she passed away . . . early that afternoon.' "

"Grandma," interrupted Sarah, "was she an angel when she came to your house on Christmas Eve, then? Was she your guardian angel?"

"Yes, darling, I believe she became my guardian angel that night. After that day, my mother never worried about Ralph again. She put the lock of Ralph's hair into the cedar hope chest along with the beautiful boy angel. Every once in awhile, I would see her open the box and take the angel out. She would hold him up to the light and a gentle smile would lift her face, for she too now had a guardian angel.

"Mother spent the rest of her life continuing to serve others and when my mother died she gave the cedar hope chest with the red velvet lining to me. She also gave me her crystal angel."

Grandma rocked back and forth for a moment as

they both looked at the little red buckets up on the shelf.

"Grandma, do you still have the angels?" Sarah was intent on the answer to her question.

"I only have one now. I gave the little girl angel to your mother when she was ten years old. Next year she will give it to you when you turn ten. But I still have the hope chest with the red buckets carved into the sides, and I still have the boy angel. Would you like to see them?"

"Oh, Grandma, yes, could I please?" Sarah pleaded.

"Surely, my little earth angel, let's just take the bread out of the oven first, shall we?"

The End